THE GIRL FROM GRETNA GREEN

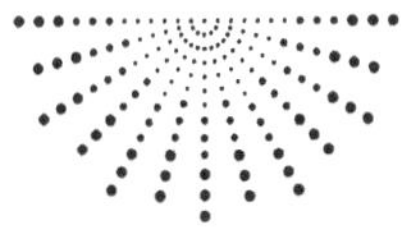

CHARITY MCCOLL

PUREREAD.COM

CONTENTS

A SNIFF OF SCANDAL

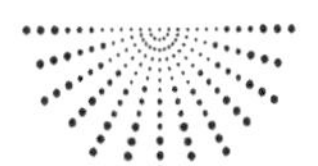

The servants of the earl of Langley believed that there was no better master in all of England. His cook Mrs. Deets often said that she would not have left his Lordship's service if the Prince Regent himself were to have asked her. She was so fond of saying this that she seemed to consider it a real possibility. If His Highness had indeed been in the habit of paying visits to gentlemen's residences with the design of seducing servants to his own household, he would have found the cook, of Sir Giles Kensington, as staunch and steadfast as any in London.

It was a testament to this loyalty that when she heard the shocking news about Lady Annabella Harcourt, Mrs. Deets managed to refrain from shouting it on the streets. She only told Mrs. Hodges when she called over from next door with a coveted recipe, swore that good woman to secrecy, and scolded the skivvy when she gave some hint of the affair to the visiting butcher, before bustling out into the yard to tell him herself. Mrs. Deets was a large woman with a small face and smaller eyes, and the maids and footmen of Cheltenham Place lived in fear of her wrath. Even the butler Mr. Pearce, who spoke as well as any gentleman in White's or Boodle's, was not immune to her scolding.

On the present occasion, he leapt to his feet with the other servants as Mrs. Deets returned from her conference with the butcher to a general scraping of chairs. "Alfred! I expect you're not too high and mighty to bring the tea tray up to the library, or do you expect Sir Giles to come down here and serve himself?" The footman shook his head and seized up the silver tray with his white gloves. "Martha! Is the fire lit in his Lordship's chamber?"

"That won't be necessary," Mr. Pearce said, with an apologetic cough as Mrs. Deets's small eyes landed on him. "He will be making for Gretna Green soon."

"Isn't it *romantic*?" exclaimed Martha, clasping her hands together.

"It ain't romantic, it's plain foolish," Mrs. Deets contradicted. "But I *said* no good would come of the master sending Lady Annabella to school. Didn't I say it, Alfred?" She raised her voice so that the footman could hear her, and a moment later, his voice came floating down the servants' staircase.

"That you did, Mrs. Deets, that you did."

"That French woman," the cook continued in normal tones, bustling over to the oven. "Madam whatever-you-like…"

"Madame de Fournay," Martha supplied importantly. Since her great aunt had married a baronet, she never ceased to tell the other servants, she was deemed the expert on the pronunciation of foreign names.

"… has been filling the girls' heads with nonsense, and letting them run wild in the country. Tis no wonder Lady Annabella has eloped with the stable l– d - help me with the scones, Martha. No, stay a minute…" Mrs. Deets's head turned at the sound of a door slamming upstairs, and she dropped her voice to a whisper while Mr. Pearce seized up a paper and pretended he was not listening. "Better go up and see what you can find out."

Alfred the footman was coming out of the library when Martha reached it, the untouched tea tray in his hands. He shook his head significantly at her, and a moment later, the master himself had burst out the door. He was clad in his waistcoat and cravat, and was distractedly putting on his gloves as he issued orders. "... cannot withstand a moment's delay. Tell Mr. Pearce to bring the carriage around. I shall be gone for several days - perhaps a week. It is impossible to know. Ah! Martha."

The head housemaid dipped into a curtsey as the earl's dark blue eyes landed on her, and scolded herself for the deep blush that was spreading in her cheeks; she had served many masters in her time, but none quite so young or handsome as Sir Kensington. It was something she felt she would never get used to. "Will you inform Mrs. Deets that the Lady Clarissa will be residing here in my absence? I trust you can arrange everything between yourselves." Sir Giles took a breath, and then set off down the corridor at a quick stride. The maid and footman followed after him, exchanging glances, and were only stopped at the bottom of the main staircase by a withering look from Mr. Pearce, who was holding the master's cloak and hat.

"The carriage is outside, my lord." His voice echoed through the wide hallway. Sir Giles nodded, and clapped the butler on the shoulder. "Thank you, Mr. Pearce. Now I must be gone." A whirl of his cloak, a series of quick, hurrying steps, and he was as good as his word. Martha could not resist rushing to the landing window to look out: it stood half open, and she heard the rolling carriage wheels, saw a gleam of lamplight in the window, and the master's dark head framed in it, as he departed through the growing dusk of London.

MRS. NOT MISS

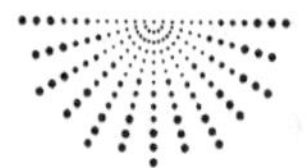

Sir Giles Kensington, the seventh earl of Langley, was not accustomed to being kept waiting.

The long journey from town had frayed his nerves past repair; he had enjoyed no sleep in the past few days, his mind filled with visions of horror involving the Lady Annabella and her mysterious lover. And now that he had stopped for refreshment in the White Hart inn a few miles outside Gretna Green, nothing seemed to be going his way. The slatternly proprietress had promised to make inquiries on his behalf regarding his missing ward; yet that had been a half-hour ago, and she had not reappeared.

He felt inclined to knock his forehead against the wood of the table as he considered his predicament.

He had always conducted himself with the utmost decorum and discretion; why was it that the rest of his family showed themselves incapable of doing the same? Only last week he had been called upon to resolve a dispute between his younger sister and her new husband over the purchase of a pair of nankin boots; last month Randolph had run up a pile of debts over a game of faro in Oxford and come to *him* for help, and at Candlemas, Anthony had written to him seeking permission to make yet another penniless young woman the lady of Huntingsend. In each case, Sir Giles had done his duty. The lovers had been reconciled, the debts repaid, and the permission refused, but all the same, it did take its toll.

His older sister Clarissa was the only one among his siblings on whom he could rely, and even then, with her husband away at sea she had begun to interfere in the affairs of her bachelor brother, so that Sir Giles was not altogether sorry for the crisis that had taken him out of her reach for a little while. It was only a pity, he reflected as he looked down at his untouched dinner, that this particular crisis should involve the very person whom his influence had never been able to touch.

A few feet away, the landlady of the White Hart peered out from the backroom, wiped her hands on her apron, and then hissed, "Girl! *Girl!*" She was a sallow woman, with narrow eyes, a long, thin face and prominent front teeth.

The pretty serving maid, absently polishing a glass behind the bar, took a moment to look around. When she did, her dark blue eyes landed on her mistress and widened. "I-I'm sorry Miss Higgenbotham, I didn't hear you…"

"*Mrs.,*" the landlady corrected peevishly. She came right up to the girl and said in a carrying whisper, "Go and serve that gentleman over there."

The maid glanced over at the tall young man sitting in the corner of the room, a glass of port before him. He was looking expectantly at them. "Some fine lord," the landlady went on. "Looking for his sister. He asked me to make inquiries, but I clean forgot - you know how I have so much on my mind. Best not tell him that…"

"Not my sister," the man corrected, unfolding himself from his seat. The landlady gave a scandalised gasp. As he made his way towards them, "I could not help overhearing - my apologies for the impertinence. The lady in question is my ward: Lady

Annabella Harcourt. She is thought to have passed near here. Auburn hair, green eyes; she is a striking enough person that I daresay you would have noticed her."

"My Douglas says green eyes is unlucky," said Mrs. Higgenbotham to her serving maid in an undertone. The gentleman"s expression did not change. Raising her voice to a normal level again, "Ain't you a little young to have a ward?" As his dark eyebrows rose, she added hastily, "My lord?"

The serving maid ducked her head, blushing for her mistress, but the gentleman replied calmly, "I have been head of my family since my father passed away twelve years ago. Had he lived longer, the lady I seek would still be in his care, and I imagine he would have been more fitted for the task. However, the duty now falls to me."

"Of course, of course," Mrs. Higgenbotham murmured, sucking a breath through her teeth. Her long, narrow eyes had lit with interest, and she seemed on the point of inquiring further when the maid, with a hasty glance at her mistress, interjected,

"We've not seen her. My lord."

Sir Giles Kensington glanced at the serving maid, and inclined his head. "Thank you. Then I shall be on my way." He was turning about when something struck him, and looking back, he frowned. "What is your name?"

"Sal Higgenbotham at your service, m'lord - "

"Not *you*," Sir Giles said wearily. "I was addressing this young woman." He looked at the maid more closely than he had before, taking in her dark blue eyes, the black hair, the round chin. It had to be a coincidence - but how was it that she could remind him so much of…

"Adelaide Coventry, sir," the maid said, bowing her head again. As she did so, Sir Giles's eyes alighted on something else.

"Where did you get that necklace?"

It was a stag against a filigree design: the same coat-of-arms which adorned his mother's carriage back in the country house in Langley, whose origins she had explained to him countless times when he was a boy. But how could it be that a young serving girl was wearing the crest of the Buchanan family?

Composing himself with an effort, for the two women were still staring at him from behind the bar, he resolved on making one last inquiry. This ought to settle it all, Sir Giles told himself, as he asked of the young girl, "Have you ever been to London?"

Adelaide Coventry's eyes widened in surprise. "London! Never, my lord."

"Never!" Sir Giles repeated, staggered. "But how…"

"My lord." Turning, he saw the coachman standing at the door. He looked sad and dejected. "I've looked all over the village and there's no sign of her Ladyship."

"No matter. We shall keep looking." Sir Giles sighed. "Good day to you both." Tipping his hat at the women, he grabbed up his cloak.

"Wait just a minute." The voice of the landlady drifted after him as he was stepping over the threshold. He looked around to see that she had come around the partition, her face screwed up as though she were trying to remember something. "Green eyes and red hair, did you say?"

"Yes," Sir Giles said slowly. "Might you have seen something of her after all?"

"I b'lieve we have. Don't you remember, Adelaide? The fine lady what came in earlier with a dark gentleman?" Sal Higgenbotham gave the serving girl a nudge.

"Y-yes ma'am, I- I remember now."

"We'd better come with you, then, my lord, hadn't we." Mrs. Higgenbotham folded her arms. "To act as your guides."

The earl of Langley exchanged a glance with his coachman, who shrugged. "Very well. Lead the way."

3

NEW FRIENDS

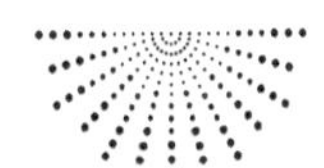

Sir Giles Kensington was only thirty years old, and where other gentlemen his age might have studied law or medicine or the church, he studied his family. They were his profession, and since the age of eighteen, they had never afforded him more than a moment's repose. For even supposing all of his siblings blighted from the earth, and all their troubles with them, there would still remain that eternal thorn in his side, the orphaned daughter of his father's old comrade Harcourt.

When he first met her, she had been only a child, and a sweet one by all appearances. As then she was only eight, and did not appear likely to trouble anyone, Sir Giles had placed her in the country estate

Huntingsend, where she might eventually prove a useful companion to his mother. A governess was engaged, and gave in her notice within the week. Within two weeks, the stern housekeeper had been reduced to tears: within a month, Lady Louisa was begging him to place Annabella elsewhere. The young ward was sent to stay with Lady Clarissa and her husband in town, where, for a time, she was contented.

London, with all of its varieties and diversions, had suited her altogether much better. In those days Sir Giles often visited Camden Place, and tested the child on her lessons: she certainly had no shortage of sense, and her accomplishments grew with her age. And although she had an impertinent way of calling him 'Kensington' as if she were one of the gentlemen who fenced with him in Bond Street, and often presumed to advise him - *she*, advise *him*! - on everything from the new ha-ha he planned to build on the estate to how many holidays he ought to give his servants, on the whole, Sir Giles thought her a good girl, who, with her advantages of beauty, temper and fortune, was sure to make a fine match one day.

It was a pity, Sir Giles reflected, as he regarded the Scottish countryside spread out before him, that things had turned out the way they had.

"I really am beginning to think," he ventured to say as the carriage rolled over a bump in the road, "that you never saw Lady Annabella at all. We have been travelling all day, and you have not been able to tell me one useful thing."

"Well, I never!" Sal Higgenbotham, lounging in the seat opposite, lit up with outrage. "Tell him, Adelaide! Tell him what we saw!"

But Adelaide was occupied in looking out the window and admiring the scenery. "How lovely! Look, Miss Higgenbotham!"

"Mrs.," Sal corrected peevishly, and glancing over her companion's shoulder, grunted. "Hmph. Seen plenty like it."

Sir Giles, who had been watching Adelaide curiously, now peered out himself. Behind them rose umber hills and beyond glittered the waters of a lake. The sight of all that rustic beauty made him feel a little sentimental. It made him inclined to think that perhaps Lady Annabella had *not* been to blame in this whole affair. After all, was not the founder of

Madame de Fournay's Academy for Female Education and Deportment, for all her respectability and prestige - French? And, with such notions of love and romance necessitated by this state of being, might she not have been a corrupting influence on her students? At any rate, it was clear that she had not been wise in choosing the servants of her establishment.

Now, Sir Giles settled on the real villain of the piece: Annabella's abductor, whose figure had by now taken on Byronic proportions, and who grew in his imagination less like the humble stable lad that had first crossed it and more like a dark-eyed, silver-tongued libertine described by Sal Higgenbotham with every passing hour. Somewhere along the way he had acquired a gig, which he drove with long hair streaming out behind him, gnashed his teeth and whipped his horses into a frenzy and foamed at the mouth while Annabella shrieked and swooned beside him.

Never mind that he had never seen his ward so much as flinch at a raised voice; never mind that it had become clear Mrs. Higgenbotham had been making it all up; the horrid picture settled itself in Sir Giles's mind. His hand edged towards his overcoat as the carriage jolted again, the inside pocket of which contained a silver pistol. He had never used it; its very existence could not be separated from the fact of his father's passing, for Lord Rupert Kensington had died twelve years ago using that very same pistol in a duel. Now, it seemed that Sir Giles might share his father's fate. That was, if they should ever find Lady Annabella.

Adelaide was exclaiming in delight. "I say, they're having a picnic! Can't we get out for just a minute!"

"Remember yourself, girl," Sal Higgenbotham snapped. "Lord Kensington is a busy man."

But Sir Giles smiled, and raised his hand to rap his knuckles on the roof of the carriage. A moment later, they had come to a halt, and he stepped out, steadying himself before he reached back. "Come, Adelaide."

The young girl's eyes widened as they met his, and then she shyly took his hand and stepped out, lifting her skirts a little so that they would not be sprayed with mud. They had stopped a little way from the lakeshore, and the sound of laughter drifted towards them on the warm air. Down the green slope, Sir Giles could see a lady sitting on the grass, laughing and clutching her hat as a boy splashed about in the water.

"You have worked in the White Hart for some time, I take it?" he said as they began to walk.

"Since I can remember." Adelaide glanced behind her, where the grumbling landlady was following behind them. "Mrs. Higgenbotham has been very good to me. She raised me by hand."

"Raised you? Then your parents are not living?"

"I know nothing of them." Adelaide Coventry looked down, and Sir Giles's eyes widened. They were coming up to the pair by the lakeside now, and he lowered his voice.

"Forgive me, Adelaide, I do not wish to press, but…"

"Kensington!"

Slowly, the seventh Earl of Langley turned and saw the object of his quest a mere few paces away. She was sitting alone, only a coverlet between her and the grass, a basket of wrapped food at her feet. The sun gleamed in her red hair, which was partly loose under her straw hat, the escaping tendrils framing her heart-shaped face. A shawl around her shoulders completed the picture, so that she looked the very ideal of Nature. Sir Giles thought he must be dreaming. For a moment he was at a loss for words. "You… you…"

"What brings you here?" his ward continued, as she rose to her feet and curtsied. "I hope Madame hasn't been making a fuss about my leaving. I *did* leave a note. And Tom was with me, so I was quite safe." She laughed, looking over her shoulder at the boy splashing in the water. "Tom! Tom, come meet my guardian, Sir Giles Kensington!"

Grinning from ear to ear, the boy came up onto the muddy shore, thrusting out a hand. He was all freckles and limbs, and did not look likely to have ever owned a gig. "Tom Turner at your service, sir. I work in the stables at the Academy." Meeting Sir Giles's gaze, his face dropped, and he lowered his hand again. "Or - I did, until..."

"Until you eloped with my ward?"

"You must forgive Kensington's manners," Annabella said to the stable boy. "They are not quite what they should be." Turning to Sir Giles, she folded her arms. "Now, you must not blame Tom, Kensington. He's been a perfect gentleman, and..."

"Pardon me, what age are you?" Sir Giles spluttered.

"He's twelve," Annabella said impatiently. "Now, Kensington, as I was saying, it was all my idea. There's this horrid girl in the Academy, you see, Prudence Wood, and she dared me to do something shocking. I couldn't very well say no, could I?"

"Miss Wood *is* horrid, sir," Tom Turner supplied gravely. "She whips her horse for fun."

"Indeed." Sir Giles could hardly contain his amazement. "So it was a noble quest, after all."

"Precisely." Lady Annabella looked delighted. "I knew you would see reason." Her eyes slid past Sir Giles. "And who are your companions?"

"This is Adelaide Coventry." The servant girl's eyes had been fixed on the young lady in awe throughout her conversation with Sir Giles, and now she curtsied deeply. Her mistress, however, did not, pressing forward as she shook a finger at Lady Annabella.

"You're a very wicked girl."

"And that," Sir Giles added, "is Sal Higgenbotham."

"I *like* her." Lady Annabella Harcourt's green eyes danced as she looked back at Sir Giles. "Isn't it lovely to make new friends?"

Madame Genevieve de Fournay might have erred in her estimation of the danger into which her stable boy was capable of placing the young lady who had been in her charge, and on hearing from Sir Giles Kensington by the morning post the next day, she was ready to admit her mistake. What she was not ready to do, however, was the one thing on which he had counted as a certainty: accept his ward back to her school.

There was nothing else for it but to bring Annabella back to town with him, but Sir Giles was reluctant to do so when the question of the Coventry girl was still lingering in his mind.

After their adventure together, the landlady of the White Hart inn had not been expecting the fine lord to linger about the place for as long as he did. Yet there he remained, morning, noon and night, always watching her Adelaide with close attention. Sal Higgenbotham did not like to interfere, but with her Douglas always out for the count upstairs - "sleeping it off", some might have said, but Mrs. Higgenbotham did not use such indelicate expressions - she had assigned herself as Adelaide Coventry's sole protector, and when Sir Giles Kensington at last made his vile intentions known, she was moved to speak.

"Now, my lord, this here is a respectable establishment, and Adelaide, for all we don't know where she came from, is a respectable girl."

"I am aware of that," Sir Giles said wearily, "but she is of great interest to me for reason of her -"

"I'm sure she is, my lord, I'm sure she is." Sal Higgenbotham nodded sagely. "A bonny face she has, and you're not the first fine gentleman to notice, let me tell you, but for all that she is a respectable girl, and I've heard what goes on down in town - with those gambling dens and godless men and Lord Byron…"

"Have you ever been to London, Mrs. Higgenbotham?"

"No, indeed!" The landlady's face had brightened with interest, as though a sudden idea had struck her. "Of course, if I was to go with you, I'm sure there could be nothing amiss."

This was the very situation Sir Giles had hoped to avoid. Putting a hand to his forehead, he considered for a moment. To leave the girl here would be to leave a mystery unsolved, and that was something he could not countenance. But to spirit her away without a chaperone would incite scandal, a thing which he had only narrowly avoided yesterday. He sighed. Was it his fate always to run from scandal to scandal?

Mrs. Higgenbotham was still talking. "... my Douglas would look after the place, and I'm sure I'd keep your young lady in check, too..."

"Very well," Sir Giles Kensington said. "Very well, Mrs. Higgenbotham. We depart tomorrow at first light."

4

OUT OF THE FRYING PAN

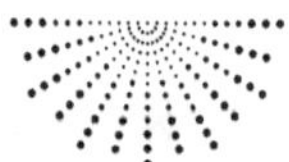

Lady Clarissa Shaftesbury was most thankful for the safe return of her dear Annabella to Cheltenham Place, and when the whole affair had been disclosed to her, she was more inclined to let it slide than her brother Giles liked. It was the result of high spirits and the monotony of school; she herself had done many similar things in her youth, before she had met her Admiral, and on the whole, she thought that the less said about the whole thing, the better.

The servants of No. 12, on the other hand, took a different view. Their master had returned from Gretna Green with three new servants in tow; had given no account of them before he had deposited them below stairs, and so the butler Mr. Pearce had been left to puzzle the matter out. Orders issued over the next few days confounded things further: why was this young dark-haired girl to be assigned to Lady Annabella as her maid? What right had this Higgenbotham woman to insist on being addressed as a matron when by, her own admission, she and her man had never "tied the knot" (an expression which Mr. Pearce abhorred), and to appoint herself as assistant cook when she had never even heard of a syllabub?

But it was Tom Turner who provided the greatest mystery: this simple young lad who had somehow led the sweet Annabella down the road of sin. Mr. Pearce and Alfred often peered out the hall window at the boy as he brought the horses around from the mews, and attributed him with evil designs when he came into the kitchen to ask Mrs. Deets for a lump of sugar.

"You know what you have to do, of course," said Lady Clarissa to Sir Giles one evening, about a week after he had saved his ward from scandal. They were entertaining some friends of the Admiral, who now sat around a table engaged in a game of whist which both brother and sister had managed to avoid.

"I'm sure you are going to tell me, in any case," was the response, and Lady Clarissa simply smiled as she put down her work.

"You must find Annabella a husband."

Sir Giles raised his eyebrows, and directed a pointed look across the room, to where his ward was playing a concerto that was rather too loud for the headache that pounded at his temples. "What man is to have the misfortune?"

"There are plenty of fine young men out there who would be glad to undertake the challenge. She is rich, pretty, accomplished - " at her brother's snort, " - yes, even *you* must see that. We all know she is headstrong..."

"I was not aware," interposed her brother dryly.

Lady Clarissa leaned forward, her expression solemn now, and said in quieter tones, "But how can you expect otherwise, Giles? The girl has been moved about her whole life. She has never had anyone to guide her. *I* have tried my best, of course, and the Admiral always loved her like a father, but such efforts cannot take the place of parents."

"Is nothing to be said of *my* efforts?"

"Your efforts," his sister said composedly, "have certainly been great, but Giles, you're simply too young to be a proper guardian to her; I have always said it. And you do not know her well enough. If only Father had not died…"

"However, he did," Sir Giles said abruptly, pushing back his chair as applause sounded around the room, "And I must do my best in his place." He was beginning to rise to his feet when his sister laid a hand on his arm.

"Annabella should be settled," she said quietly. "Soon. If we are to avoid another scandal."

Sir Giles looked at his sister a moment, and then sighed. "What needs to be done?"

Across the drawing room, Lady Annabella smiled and curtsied as applause rang around her, while inside, her mind was working quickly. What were her guardian and Clarissa discussing? She had no doubt that it involved herself, as she had caught them watching her several times throughout the performance, and yet they had looked so grave that she was sure it must be something unpleasant. In the midst of her reflections, the footman - whose name she could not recall, but whose expression always made him appear to be suffering from some acute indigestion - entered and bent to address his master.

Kensington looked surprised. "Why, *now*, of course!" Annabella heard him say, and then, with a glance towards his guests, who had turned from their table expectantly at the interruption, he raised his voice. "Tea will be brought up presently, as I know speculation is thirsty work."

There was a ripple of laughter at these words, and the footman looked even more pained than usual as he backed out of the room. Annabella glanced at the clock above the mantlepiece. It was past nine: she knew that Cheltenham Place kept very strict hours, and tea would normally have been served and cleared by now. Was there some delay?

"My lady, you must favour us with another ballad," one of her guardian's guests was saying, and another young man was advancing towards the piano to offer his services as a page-turner when Annabella shut her piano book, made her excuses, and left her astounded audience behind.

Outside, all was quiet in the long, echoing corridors of Cheltenham Place, but Annabella pressed on, curious. She caught sight of her maid crossing the hall. "Adelaide! Is something the matter downstairs?"

Her maid turned a pale face towards her, startled at the echo of her mistress's voice. "Oh! Lady Annabella, something dreadful has happened - but..." with a fearful glance at the door that led to the servants' staircase, "Mr. Pearce says we're not supposed to say anything."

Her mistress considered for a moment, then took her maid's arm. "All right. Lead the way."

"My lady…"

Deaf to her maid's protests, Lady Annabella Harcourt descended the servants' staircase, lifting her skirts to aid her passage. There was a general cry of alarm as she entered the servants' hall, with many shocked 'my ladys', all of which she ignored as she followed Adelaide Coventry into the kitchen. Part of the room was clouded by smoke, and the housemaid was arguing with the footman.

"We can't do anything about it, Alfred! Nothing's ready!"

"What has happened?" Lady Annabella broke in, and they both turned with wide eyes to regard her. It was Sal Higgenbotham who answered, rising from where she had been seated by the fireplace.

"She's only gone and walked off the job." A kind of triumph gleamed in her narrow eyes, as she indicated the voluminous apron that had been slung over one of the chairs. "Mrs. Deets. Isn't it shocking?"

"Don't pretend it ain't *your* doing!" The housemaid's eyes flashed in anger, and she turned to Lady Annabella in appeal. "Since the master brought her here she's been nothing but trouble, my lady. Acting like she owns the kitchen."

"Martha," the footman said warningly, as Mrs. Higgenbotham drew herself up in fiery indignation.

"I never did! And his Lordship will have you all out the door once he hears about this, you mark my words…"

"He'll do no such thing," Lady Annabella said calmly, rolling up her puffed sleeves, and they all turned to stare at her. "Because he won't hear about it. Now, what needs to be done? Martha?"

The head housemaid blinked, as though coming out of a trance. "The… the sandwiches aren't cut…"

"Very good. I will take care of that." With quick, light steps, Annabella went to the chair, seized up Mrs. Deets' discarded apron, and, to the horror of the onlookers, tied it over her green silk gown. As she was tying the back, she looked up at the servants around her, and gave one of her mischievous, merry smiles. "There's no need to look like that. I did this sort of thing all the time in school."

"It's not right, my lady..." the footman began, grimacing, but she cut across him.

"Alfred, you had better bring the ices up before Sir Kensington calls in the Bow Street runners. Martha, go and find Mrs. Deets. Reason with her - I'm sure she can't have gone far. Adelaide, you will help me, and... "As the tavern keeper's wife advanced towards her, "Mrs. Higgenbotham, I think *you* have done enough."

It was not long before the kitchen had been restored to its former order: everyone occupied by doing their own tasks, and the back door thrown open to let out the smoke and let in the butler, whose directions to Tom Turner regarding His Lordship's horses were abruptly cut short by the scene which greeted him.

"Oh, hello, Mr. Pearce," said the master's ward cheerfully, as she sliced the last triangle of sandwiches. "You missed all the fun. Could you pass me the parsley?"

Ten minutes later, the tea tray was brought up to the drawing room. Lady Annabella Harcourt slipped in the door shortly afterwards, with not a hair out of place nor a wrinkle in her gown, and smiled at

Clarissa as she stepped forward to pour the tea for their hungry guests.

Sir Giles Kensington was blissfully unaware of the near disaster that had threatened the tranquility of his household anew. All he knew was that there had been a short delay in tea, but that it finally arrived, Annabella returned, his guests were happy, and all had come right in the end. His sister was now too occupied in her conversation with the captain's wife to continue nagging him, and, in short, his mood was soon so improved as to induce him to actually admire his ward's piano playing.

5

JULIET AND ROSALINE

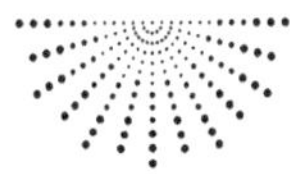

Amid the concerns surrounding his ward's future, Sir Giles Kensington had not forgotten about Adelaide Coventry. Upon his return to town, he had made inquiries among the various branches of the Buchanans he knew to be settled there, but to no avail. Clarissa had been equally unhelpful; she only admitted, when confronted with the appearance of Adelaide, that there was a resemblance, but showed a remarkable incuriosity about the rest. So her brother was at last driven to do what he had dreaded: visit his mother.

Lady Louisa Kensington had long avowed her distaste for town, and so her sons and daughters always came to her whenever they wished to renew their maternal bond. The family seat was in the parish of Langley, a good hundred miles from

London, but Sir Kensington was well used to the journey. He started from Cheltenham Place at dawn, and the sun was high in the sky by the time his carriage came up the drive.

The appeal of Huntingsend lay more in the gardens and lawns surrounding it: the building itself was plain enough, and its favoured rooms were in the back of the house, facing the south orchard and pretty, sunlit avenues. One such avenue was overlooked from the window of the drawing room into which Sir Giles was shown by the housekeeper.

"You're here? Good," was the Dowager Countess's greeting to her son. A diminutive, sharp-eyed woman, she was seated by the window, her pug sleeping in her lap. She offered one dry cheek to Sir Giles as he approached her chair.

"Mother, I apologise that I did not give notice of my coming, but I was in a hurry to see you."

"He's got another one," his mother interrupted, without looking around.

"Who?" Sir Giles frowned at his mother, then followed her gaze as she pointed out the window. Outside on the avenue, his brother was promenading with a young woman. The youngest child of the Kensington clan had the same dark blue eyes and black hair as his brother, but that was where the similarities ended. He was thin as a rake where Giles was broad-shouldered, and wore a pair of round spectacles.

"Who do you think she is?" the Dowager Countess said, as the female companion came into closer view. She had a round, plain face, but was colourfully dressed. "The agent's niece. A Miss Hale. Hasn't got a penny. They were introduced at the Parsonage the other day. Anthony must not have been wearing his glasses."

"Mother, that's not very courteous," Sir Giles reprimanded, but Lady Louisa merely pursed her lips and gave her pug a firm pat on the head as Anthony and Miss Hale disappeared among the trees again. "Mother, may I present someone to you?" Taking her silence as permission, he turned his head towards the door, and called, "Adelaide? You may come through now."

Adelaide Coventry entered the drawing room. She was clad in the black of her lady's maid garb, and crimsoned as she bent her knees in a curtsey. "My lady."

"Girl," Lady Louisa said, glancing at her, "Go and fetch back my son. Tell him it's nearly teatime."

Adelaide Coventry's forehead creased for a moment in confusion, and then, with another curtsey, she went out again. Sir Giles stared at his mother, struck dumb for a moment. "Why did you…"

"I don't want him catching cold," Lady Louisa said placidly. "Anthony has weak lungs, you know."

"Mother…" Sir Giles shook his head in disbelief. "Mother, *that* was the young woman I wanted to present to you."

"Who, the servant?" the Dowager Countess said as the black-clad figure of Adelaide appeared through the window on the avenue, hurrying over the grass.

Sir Giles opened his mouth, then closed it again. He settled into a chair across from his mother, steepled his fingers around his chin, and at last resumed, "Mother, she *is* a servant, but we do not know her origins: I thought that perhaps you might be able to shed some light…"

"What shall I do about him, Giles?" His mother sighed, and looked out the window, where Anthony had once again become visible, now in conference with Adelaide. "I try to tell him that there are so many fortune hunters out there, but he never listens. He has such a warm heart. Like myself."

"Perhaps a profession would help," her son suggested, surrendering his end of the conversation at last.

"A profession?" Outraged, the Dowager Countess swung her head around to stare at him. The movement startled her pug out of his sleep, and the creature blinked at Sir Giles with milky eyes. "He *has* a profession! He manages the estate!"

The door opened, and the steward was announced. "My pardon for interrupting, your Ladyship, but I wanted to consult you on the rents to be collected tomorrow."

Lady Louisa produced a pair of spectacles, and looked over the scroll that the steward held before her, nodding briskly. "Yes - yes, that all looks to be in order. Thank you, Brandon."

"You were saying, Mother?" Sir Giles said flatly, when the steward had left.

"Oh Giles, don't be droll. Anthony works very hard." His mother peered out the window again. "What *can* be keeping him?"

"He certainly gets his daily exercise." Then Sir Giles sighed. "Mother, I didn't come here to argue about this. I came here on business, and because it is important, I am going to ask you again. Her name is Adelaide Coventry, and she wears around her neck the family crest of the Buchanans. It was found with her, along with gold and a letter, when she was just a baby, outside the White Hart inn near Gretna Green. Now, is it possible that one of your brothers might have - well - had an indiscretion?"

The Dowager Countess was silent for a moment, her veined hands winding around the fur of her pug. Then, abruptly, she stood, putting her pet down, and her eyes flashed a warning. "Do not speak of this matter to me again. Now, I am going to find my son."

Outside on the avenue, a profound change had just occurred. Lord Anthony Kensington was in love - again. He had known it since he had seen the dark-haired, blue-eyed beauty come tiptoeing out to fetch him back, ever since he had heard her softly speak those immortal words,

"My lord, your mother is calling for you."

Anthony took off his spectacles, wiped them on his sleeve and gazed at Adelaide Coventry. Then he dropped them with a flourish, and pressed a hand to his heart. "Did my heart love till now? Forswear it, sight! For I never saw true beauty till this night."

Miss Hale gasped and clapped her hands, unaware that she had already been forgotten. "Shakespeare! How divine!"

"Anthony!" The call echoed through the trees; the lord of Huntingsend started, and then, bowing to both Rosaline and Juliet, retrieved his broken spectacles and ran back to his mother.

6

ROUND AND ROUND

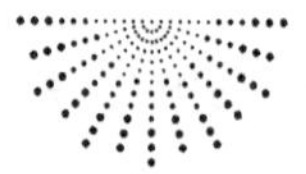

Lord Anthony Kensington was most sorry to find his brother and his pretty companion departing from Huntingsend so soon; the Dowager Countess was a little sorry, for she had hoped for a third person to make up their quadrille table, and Sir Giles was not at all. He spent the entirety of the journey back to London glaring out the window of the carriage. Adelaide Coventry, seated directly across from him, watched his face anxiously. Beside her, the maid Martha, who had come with them as a chaperone, kept demure silence.

It was, of course, unsurprising that his mother had been unable to tell him anything useful. She had always been reluctant to oblige him in any regard. What troubled him, however, was her reaction when he had mentioned the possibility of an indiscretion: it was almost as though she were fearful, as though she were indeed hiding some truth from him.

All was dark when, after a jolting journey through the dirt of London, they found themselves in the quiet of Cheltenham Place. A light rain was starting to fall. Adelaide and Martha were drooping with tiredness, and Sir Giles handed them over to Mr. Pearce's care as he stepped out of the carriage. He strode into No. 12, hung his cloak in the vestibule, crossed the tiled hall and advanced up the grand stairs. The prospect of an evening of quiet contemplation spent in the library stretched before him.

He had not been sitting down at his desk five minutes when a knock came on the door. Sir Giles dropped his forehead onto his hands, dragged them down his face, and then, straightening in his chair again, "Enter!" His eyebrows rose as he saw his visitor. "Mrs. Deets?"

The cook of Cheltenham Place shuffled in the door, looking most out of place as she said to the floor, "My lord, I am sorry to disturb you at this late hour, but I wish to hand in my notice."

"I beg your pardon?"

"My notice, sir," Mrs. Deets repeated. "Certain - changes - in the household since your return from Gretna Green, sir…"

"You mean Sal Higgenbotham," Sir Giles said, with a sigh. His cook looked up at him for the first time. "You may speak plainly, Mrs. Deets. After all, you have been in the family for - how long?"

"Nigh on five-and-twenty years, my lord," Mrs. Deets said, and she lifted her chin and her eyes shone with pride. "I was your mother's head housemaid in Huntingsend when you were still in long clothes."

Sir Giles laughed, the sound surprising himself and his cook in equal measure. "That's right. Well, Mrs. Deets." Assuming a solemn expression once more, "I know as well as you do how trying that Higgenbotham woman can be. But let me assure you her presence here will not continue for much longer."

Mrs. Deets still did not appear satisfied. Looking down at the floor again, she said, "But, my lord, if I'm unable to carry out my duties, I must leave. At dinner tonight…"

"I don't need to know," Sir Giles interrupted firmly. 'I'm sure that whatever occurred, you acted rightly, and carried out your duty in the end. And that is what we all need to do, Mrs. Deets. Our duty, no matter how provoking those around us might be." As she looked up again, he held her gaze. "It is your choice, of course. But I hope you will stay with us."

"I'll think on it, my lord," his cook said reluctantly, and Sir Giles nodded. When the door was closed, he dropped his head onto his books again and cursed.

The fatigue of the day's travel was setting in, but his mind was too active for him to wish for sleep yet. With another heavy sigh, he rose from his desk, took off his coat and put it over the chair. Loosening his cravat, he left the library in his shirtsleeves, and proceeded down the corridor, towards where he could hear distant music.

"Step - step - lively step, my lady, and - jump..."

Sir Giles stepped over the threshold of the drawing room, and leaned against the doorframe to watch. Within, the furniture had been pushed back, and the pianoforte brought forward: a dancing master sat at it, alternately playing chords and calling out to his pupil, while Lady Clarissa stood nearby, clapping her hands to keep time. Annabella spun and glided before them all, a look of intense focus on her face.

She had put a chemisette over her evening gown, and wore dancing slippers.

"Don't forget to smile, Annabella, dear!" called out Lady Clarissa, and then, catching sight of her brother, "Ah! Perfect. Giles, come here."

Warily, Sir Giles advanced forward towards where his sister stood. "Is it not too late for lessons?"

"Annabella insisted," his sister said, still smiling fondly. "She so loves to dance."

"Don't fuss, Kensington," Annabella called without stopping her set. Sir Giles rolled his eyes.

"My lord." He turned to find the dancing master at his elbow. "We are in need of a gentleman to practise the final dance. Will you do us the honour?"

Sir Giles stared, glancing down at his shirtsleeves. "I - er - well, I'm not dressed…"

"Don't be foolish, Giles," said Lady Clarissa, as she gave him a gentle push forward. "Annabella needs your help."

The dancing master had taken his seat at the piano again, and slowly began to play the opening chords of a minuet. "*Eine kleine nachtmusik*, by Herr Mozart, my lord and ladies," he called over the music. "A very delicate dance, requiring graceful footwork."

Lady Annabella raised her eyebrows at Sir Giles as he joined her on the floor, as if to say, "Are you up to the task?" Up close, he could see that she was flushed with the exertion of dancing. Strands of red hair hung about her face, and her eyes were brighter than he had ever seen them before. He waited for the cue as she began to circle him, and then extended a hand.

Annabella took it. She was not wearing gloves, and as the bare skin of her palm brushed his, for a moment Sir Giles felt uncertain. Then she let go, spinning away from him. The white of her gown moved so fast it was almost dizzying; he caught hold of her again as she moved towards him, and their eyes met over their joined hands.

"Very good! Very good!" the dancing master was calling, and it briefly registered with Sir Giles that his sister had fallen completely silent.

"It seems they taught you something in that school," he said gruffly, as Annabella turned beneath his raised arm.

There she was, mocking him again! Sir Giles was so annoyed that he briefly forgot the next step of the dance. He remembered when Annabella came to a halt before him, and angrily put a hand to her waist. Her gasp was so quiet that he was not altogether sure afterwards if he had imagined it. They spun together once, twice, and then he broke away.

"Giles!" his sister admonished, as the dancing master looked up from the piano in dismay.

"Pardon me," Sir Giles said, keeping his voice even with some effort. "I am a little tired." Turning to his ward, he bowed, and gave her a kind smile. "You're doing well, Annabella."

He tried to ignore the tingling of his left hand as he strode out of the drawing room.

"My lord. My lord?"

"Yes - yes, what?" Sir Giles snapped, as he turned from the bookshelf in his library to face his butler. He had been in here for the last hour, had taken up a volume of Johnson and read two lines before putting it down again; Milton had proved similarly challenging, and he was gearing himself up to try Sterne when this particularly vexing interruption occurred.

Mr. Pearce was pale, and uncharacteristically at a loss for words as he stammered, "Er - downstairs, my lord, you had better come…"

"Don't tell me." Sir Giles Kensington slammed down Sterne and followed his butler out of the room. "It's that Higgenbotham woman again, isn't it? I do declare, if I had any inclination of the trouble she would cause..." He fell silent as a wail echoed up from the hallway, and hurried down the stairs to greet whoever it might be.

"Oh, Giles!" Lady Alicia Eaton fell into his arms, sobbing; she had not so much as taken off her cloak. "I won't go back; I *won't!*"

Utterly baffled, Sir Giles patted his youngest sister's back. Over her shoulder, he saw Mr. Pearce hurrying to close the door, which stood open to the elements; one of the maids was already cleaning up the tracks of mud that had been left on the tiled floor.

"There was some argument," Lady Clarissa told her brother quietly as they stood outside the door of their sister's room a little while later. She had risen from bed to tend to Alicia, and still wore her hair in a long braid down her back. "With Tobias. She won't give details, but she says she would prefer to join a nunnery than return to him."

Sir Giles snorted. "If they would take her." As his sister turned to glare at him, the crying of Alicia still in their ears, he sighed. "I will talk to her in the morning. Now, you should go back to bed."

After Lady Clarissa had padded away to her chamber, Sir Giles took one look at the door of his sister's bedroom, shuddered, and returned to the library with every intention of continuing his reading.

Mr. Pearce was doing his nightly rounds when he found his Lordship in the library, slumped over an open book on his desk and snoring lightly. The butler gave a small smile, placed his master's evening coat over his shoulders, and snuffed out the candle beside him.

7

A SPOT OF TROUBLE

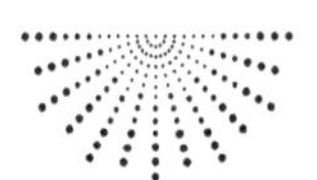

It was a nightmare. Of that much Sir Giles Kensington was certain. There was no way that morning light was already filtering in through the open curtains of the library window, when he had just rested his eyes for a moment; the distant, jaunty playing on the piano could not be real, and his brother Randolph could not possibly be beside him, shaking his shoulder and asking him for another loan.

But so it was: the light grew clearer; Sir Giles opened his scratchy eyes fully, lifted his head from the desk, and fumbled with the parchment sticking to half of his face. "What on earth…"

"Er, I'm sorry to come in on you like this, old boy," Randolph said, with a nervous laugh, "but I've run into a spot of trouble."

"Again?" Sir Giles said groggily, at last succeeding in detaching the parchment from his face. He pressed it back down onto the desk and leaned his elbow on it as he listened to his brother's long-winded explanation. Randolph Kensington, like Alicia, took more after their father's side of the family, and his blond, boyish looks often caused people to think him younger than he really was. Then again, Sir Giles mused to himself, perhaps there were other reasons for that, too.

"... so I came posthaste from Oxford, got a bit of a head start on him," Randolph concluded. "If I can get the sum together by tomorrow, Tolbrook ought to be satisfied."

"Ought to be," Sir Giles repeated dumbly. "Who is this Tolbrook fellow, in any case?"

"Oh! No one you know," his younger brother said hastily. At his older brother's look, "Well, he's often at the speculation tables - one of the best players I've ever seen..."

"I have changed my mind: I am not interested." Sir Giles rose from his desk, winced at his creaking muscles, and beckoned. "Come on."

"Er, where are we going, old boy?" Randolph said, following him out of the library.

"To see my accountant. His office should be open in about half an hour." Sir Giles consulted his pocket watch, and then tucked it back in the pocket of his creased waistcoat.

"Don't you want to change first?" his brother suggested as they came into the hall.

Sir Giles gave him another look. "The sooner we get this matter settled - thank you, Alfred - the better." Quickly buttoning his overcoat, he stepped out as Mr. Pearce threw open the doors. Randolph blinked at the strength of the morning sun as he joined him on the step.

"Aren't we taking the carriage?" He stared as his brother began to stride away. "W-wait for me!"

A brisk morning walk was among the foremost pleasures of life, or so Sir Giles Kensington believed. Randolph certainly did not share this creed, if his grumblings on their way through town were any indication, but Sir Giles paid no heed. The sun shone off wet eaves and gleamed in puddles on the streets, and his spirits lifted with every step.

The sound of distant drums reached their ears as they drew up to Mr. Forster's office at the end of Bond Street. "Wait here," said Sir Giles, and Randolph, fagged from the journey, obeyed without a word. He leaned an arm on the railing and panted as his brother climbed the steps into the townhouse.

A quarter of an hour's conference with his accountant in the stuffy offices of No. 61 Bond Street was sufficient to make the arrangements necessary for Randolph's relief, but also to evaporate Sir Giles's good humour. He emerged from the office hot and cross, his mind reeling with numbers, to find his companion vanished from his spot by the railings.

There was only a moment's alarm before he spotted him again a little way down the street, engaged in watching a military display. As Sir Giles drew up to him, Randolph exclaimed, without taking his eyes off the waving flags and polished rifles, "Splendid, isn't it?"

"That is the Longstone regiment. They are in town for a fortnight, I believe."

"Splendid!" his brother repeated, and it seemed to be all he could say on the way home, even when Sir

Giles laid before him the particulars of his meeting with Mr. Forster.

Back in Cheltenham Place, Lady Clarissa burst into Annabella's dressing room while she was finishing her hair. "They're here at last!"

With a squeal of excitement, Annabella jumped up from the vanity and followed her guardian's sister out of the room, Adelaide trailing a few steps behind. They flew down the hall, passing startled servants, and came into the drawing room, where a collection of packages had been laid out on one of the tables.

Annabella threw herself on the first one with shining eyes, and Clarissa was busying herself opening another when someone cleared their throat behind them.

The two ladies looked up guiltily to see Lady Alicia Eaton standing in the doorway. She had not bothered dressing her hair, and there were rings about her eyes as though she had been crying all night. "What… is this?"

Lady Clarissa was the first to speak. "The materials for Lady Annabella's gown have arrived from Paris." At Alicia's uncomprehending look, "She is to have her coming-out tomorrow."

"Oh." Lady Alicia pressed a hand to her heart, and appeared very moved. "How… how…"

"Lovely?" suggested Annabella with a winning smile, then her eyes widened as Alicia descended on her, seizing her hands in a fervent plea.

"How *dreadful*! Oh, Annabella, you must never marry!" As the younger woman shrank back, Alicia pressed forward, her eyes wild. "Look at me! Marriage has been my ruin!"

"Alicia," Clarissa said, in placating tones, but her sister ignored her, only growing more desperate in her pleas.

"Annabella, dear, dear Annabella, do not be deceived by all this!" She gestured at the packages around them. "The man you marry may provide for you at the beginning, but in the end…" Dropping Annabella's hands, with a look of resignation, "… in the end, it will not matter to him if you go hungry."

"I'm sure that whatever man I marry –" Annabella began, but at a warning look from Clarissa, stopped short too late. Alicia burst into fresh tears, dropping to her knees on the floor as she began to beat the carpet. Alarmed, Annabella edged away from her and looked to Clarissa, with a wince as Alicia's cries grew louder. "What are we to do?"

A soft voice spoke from the doorway, and they both turned to see Adelaide Coventry. "Your Ladyship. I might be able to help." At a gesture from Clarissa, she came forward and knelt by Alicia, putting a gentle hand on her shoulder. She spoke quietly, and Alicia, hiccupping, began to listen. The two ladies watched in wonderment.

Sir Giles Kensington was most surprised to return, with his brother in tow, to an orderly household. The hall was being aired, the maids were humming, and Alfred was polishing the portrait frames. Clarissa came up to him as he was passing the drawing room to inform him that Alicia had taken breakfast, and then retired to bed again.

"I was expecting her to be up by now," Sir Giles said in surprise. "Making a racket."

"She was," his sister said grimly. "You have that girl, Adelaide, to thank for this peace and quiet."

"Adelaide?"

"She was able to make her tranquil. I haven't the slightest idea how. But..." Lady Clarissa met her brother's gaze. "Perhaps you were right, Giles. Perhaps there *is* more to her than meets the eye." After a moment's pause, she shrugged. "She also suggested that we summon her husband. I am not so sure if *that* would be wise."

"I am beginning to think that we have no other choice," Sir Giles murmured, and as his sister walked off down the corridor, stayed where he was for a moment.

He was still pondering her words about Adelaide when he opened the drawing room door to the sound of delighted laughter. Randolph had Annabella in his arms, and was swinging her about in the air, as he had always done before when she was a child; but somehow, the sight now made something clench within Sir Giles. He watched as Randolph set his ward down with a grin, watched as she tipped her head back, still laughing, a cascade of red curls falling down her back.

"It's jolly good to see you," Randolph was saying to Annabella when his older brother came up and seized his arm.

"Randolph, a word?"

Back in the peaceful surroundings of his library, Sir Giles soon regained his composure, as he nodded to his brother to take the seat opposite his desk. "Mr. Forster informed me that the money will be made available to us no earlier than tomorrow."

"You told me this already, old boy," Randolph said easily, lounging back in his chair. "Is that why you called me in?"

"Yes - well -" a little flustered, Sir Giles shuffled through the papers on his desk and then said abruptly, "This Tolbrook fellow, who bested you. Will he be able to trace you to this residence?"

"Well - er..." Now it was Randolph's turn to be flustered. He coughed. "I had to give him an address, you see, to convince him that I would honour my word."

Slowly, Sir Giles looked up from his papers. "And you gave him this address?"

"Ah, yes, I did." Randolph laughed again. "Well, I couldn't send him to Mother, could I? And I don't think he will be much trouble, if we give him the money up front first thing tomorrow. He's not a very violent man."

"Not *very* violent?" Sir Giles said faintly.

"Only when provoked. Well, old boy -" Randolph started up from his seat. "I should really say hello to everyone, don't you think? I hear Alicia is here somewhere." He hurried out of the library, and his brother, too dumbfounded to form the right words, made no attempt to stop him.

Darkness fell over London, the rains returned, and Tom Turner, the stable lad, ran out to check on the horses. Mrs. Deets had said that there was a storm coming, and Mrs. Deets was never wrong about these things. His boyish heart was filled with compassion for the creatures shut up in the mews, but he soon found it seized by another emotion as he was greeted with the sight of a hooded rider stopped right outside No. 12, his black horse snorting and gnashing its teeth. Tom came to a stop, gulping. He remembered an old story his nurse had told him, about how the devil rode a black horse. He opened his mouth and closed it again, as the rider dismounted with a flourish and handed him the reins.

"Boy, tend to him, will you? I have come a long way tonight."

The stranger strode up the steps to the house, knocked loudly, and pushed past the butler when he opened it. "Can I help you - sir?"

"I am looking for someone," the stranger said quietly, as his wet coat dripped on the tiles of the hall. "Someone who has stolen from me."

Sir Giles and Lord Randolph stood at the top of the staircase, their eyes wide as they stared at one another in the semidarkness. Although the household had retired for the night, neither of them had been asleep when the sound of violent knocking came from downstairs.

"What do I do?" Randolph mouthed.

"Go down," Sir Giles hissed back. "Reason with him." His younger brother paled and shook his head, pressing a fist to his mouth. "Very well, then *I* will." Sighing, Randolph squared his shoulders to meet his fate.

Downstairs in the hall, the stranger threw down his hood as he approached. "Where is she?"

Randolph stopped dead. His mouth slightly open, he tilted his head and then whispered, "It's... you?"

This was the dramatic reception which Lord Anthony Kensington had been hoping for; his brother seemed very much struck with the sight of him. However, he was a little dismayed when, a moment later, Sir Giles began to laugh. "It"s only Anthony!"

8

FAMILY, DUTY, HONOUR

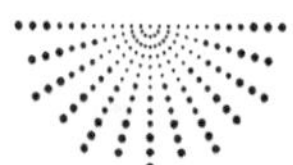

No. 12 Cheltenham Place was soon abuzz with preparations for Lady Annabella Harcourt's debut, and bursting from floor to rafter with Kensingtons.

Since there was nowhere in the house large enough to host a ball, Lady Clarissa and Sir Giles had settled on renting a room in the Almack's instead. There were many arrangements to be made, and servants and lords and ladies alike flitted between the two locations. Mrs. Deets made a cake, wrestling off Sal Higgenbotham's interference at every turn, while Tom Turner became a regular packhorse, hauling rolls of fabric and hatboxes to and fro under Mr. Pearce's direction.

The important gown was fitted at the mantua-maker's and delivered to the house on the morning of the ball, and the females of the household, servants and ladies alike, crowded into Annabella's dressing room to gaze at it.

"It will do," was Lady Annabella's proclamation, but her companions were more effusive in their praise. Only Alicia was silent. Under Adelaide's care, she had indulged in no more outbursts, but had taken to dressing in mourning colours. Now, she bent towards her maid and murmured to her, while Annabella and Clarissa exchanged apprehensive glances. Adelaide, reddening, cleared her throat. "Lady Alicia wishes me to say that though it looks very fine - the Lady Annabella should be wary of earthly pleasures... for true happiness..." She glanced uncertainly at Alicia, who hissed something at her, "...is happiness of the immortal soul."

"That is very right," Lady Annabella said with a sunny smile, and then beckoned to Adelaide. "Come, dear, and help me put this away until tonight." More quietly, as the others began to file out of the room, "You've been a wonder with her, you know."

Martha the housemaid was the last to leave. She scowled as she backed out of the room, her eyes fixed on Adelaide Coventry as the door swung closed. It was very trying, to work one's way up to becoming a lady's maid for years, only to be supplanted by a pretty little bar wench who didn't even know how to iron a lace collar. Lady Annabella was a good mistress, to be sure; no one had forgotten how she had stepped in the night Mrs. Deets nearly walked out, but this little upstart from the highlands had bewitched her, it was clear. And his Lordship had taken a fancy to her, too - oh, how unfair it was that some people had *everything*!

In the midst of these reflections, Martha did not notice the gentleman waiting at the top of the servants' staircase until he had seized her hand and pressed it to his heart. "It is *you*," he breathed.

"Let me go!" Martha tugged her hand back, and then stared up into the face of the gentleman. She could almost have taken him for Sir Giles: he had the same stormy blue eyes, and fine dark hair. But he was thinner, and his eyes were a little unfocused as they regarded her.

"I am sorry for startling you," Lord Anthony said tenderly, "but you are so beautiful that I could not help myself."

Mrs. Deets had warned her about situations like this before. Carefully, Martha began to edge her way down the step. "I've got my work to do, sir."

"I know you do." Lord Anthony made a spring forward that would have sent him headlong down the steps had Martha not caught hold of him with her sturdy arms.

"Are you all right?" she asked, a little alarmed.

"I - erm, yes. I have simply misplaced my glasses." Steadying himself, the young lord turned towards her again. "But I do not need them to look upon your beauty, my dear Adelaide."

Adelaide? Martha's face soured, and she was almost turning away when Anthony caught her hand again, and pressed it to his lips. She caught her breath, and finally, with a glance down the stairs behind her, allowed herself to be tugged back up onto the first step with him.

"You must meet me tonight," Lord Anthony whispered, clutching her shoulders. "In the kitchen garden. I will be waiting. Until then, my sweet Adelaide." With a final kiss of her hand, he swept out the door.

In the drawing room, Lady Annabella and Lord Randolph had their heads together at the pianoforte when Sir Giles burst in. "Did you hide Anthony's glasses again?" he demanded of his brother.

Randolph turned an innocent face to Giles. "And why would I do such a thing?"

"I have little time for this," Sir Giles snapped, running a hand through his hair. "You may think it a great joke, but Anthony just crashed into Alfred and almost burned him alive with tea: now Mr. Pearce is demanding an audience with me, Mrs. Deets is close to handing in her notice *again* and Mr. Eaton is downstairs, demanding to see his wife - "

"All right, hold your horses." Randolph held up his hands in a gesture of surrender. "I'll jolly well give them back." He turned to grin at Lady Annabella, but she ignored him, slipping from her seat at the piano and coming to Sir Giles's side.

"Come, Kensington," she said. He felt a light touch on his arm, and looked at her in surprise to see that her expression was serious. "We'll deal with Eaton first."

In the main parlour, Lady Alicia's husband was pacing up and down. Mr. Tobias Eaton was a small man, balding, whose spindly arms and colourless complexion that made him look as though a gust of wind would blow him away.

"I've bought her the carriage," he blurted as Sir Giles and Lady Annabella entered. They looked at him blankly. "You know, the carriage. That was what caused the row in the first place. She wanted a new carriage, and I said we couldn't afford it. Well, it's bought and paid for, and outside the door at this very moment…"

"Outside the door?" Sir Giles repeated in disbelief. "No wonder Mr. Pearce wanted to speak to me." He stepped out of the corridor and called out to his butler while Annabella regarded Mr. Eaton with sympathy.

"I'm afraid the carriage won't make her forgive you," she said sadly. "Your wife has forsaken all earthly pleasures. She wishes to join a nunnery."

"A nunnery?" Mr. Eaton repeated, blinking at her. "Earthly pleasures? What do you mean?"

"Ah, Mr. Pearce." Sir Giles addressed his butler as he approached the door of the parlour. "The carriage outside may be moved to the stables. It is a gift from Mr. Eaton for his wife."

"Very good, sir."

"Now, hold on a moment," Mr. Eaton blustered, and would have moved to stop the butler had Sir Giles not stood in his way. "Tell your man to be careful with it: that thing cost me a hundred guineas."

"A hundred guineas? My sister has a generous husband indeed."

"So I keep telling her. Now, what is this about her becoming a nun?" Mr. Eaton looked from Sir Giles to Lady Annabella, and then, seemingly uninspired by their expressions, he pushed towards the doorway again, this time succeeding in elbowing Sir Giles out of the way. "I shall talk to her myself." A moment later, they heard his voice echoing down the stairs.

"Alicia! Alicia!"

"I was unaware my house had turned into the Covent Garden market," Sir Giles murmured, and Annabella giggled. "Come on, we'd better stop him from scaring the servants."

They followed the irate husband up the stairs and showed him into the drawing room. Randolph was picking out a tune on the piano, Clarissa was embroidering, and Anthony had his chin on his hand and appeared to be gazing across at Alicia, who had her head bowed as though in prayer while Adelaide the maidservant hung about her. All of them looked up in mild surprise at the arrival of Tobias Eaton. He seemed to deflate at the sight of his wife, and was only able to manage one more apologetic, "Alicia?"

Adelaide cleared her throat. "Her Ladyship wishes me to tell you, sir, that she has taken a vow of silence."

"A vow of silence?" Mr. Eaton repeated in disbelief. "Why, she spoke just now!"

"She only speaks to Adelaide," said Anthony, as he adjusted his glasses and sent a glowing look towards the maidservant.

Now Adelaide was blushing, as she bent her ear again to hear Alicia's next commands. "My lady," she said reluctantly, "Please do not make me –" a pointed cough from her mistress silenced her protests, and she straightened once more.

"Her Ladyship says she has changed her mind about the nunnery, and now wishes for a divorce."

The horror with which these words were met was general: Clarissa went pale as death, Randolph stopped fumbling with the piano keys, and Anthony clutched at his heart, while Mr. Eaton looked as though he might faint away. Sir Giles even heard

Annabella gasp behind him. Anything which could elicit such a reaction from his ward must be shocking indeed. But the curious thing was that he himself felt no shock: he, the seventh earl of Langley, a model of decorum and good breeding, a man respected at home and abroad, a lord worthy to sit on the bench.

Yes, this was where his family's behaviour had brought him.

"That," said Sir Giles Kensington in a low, dangerous voice, "is quite enough. I have had quite enough of all of you." Turning to his youngest sister first, "Alicia, you are spoiled and selfish, and your husband is a fool to indulge your tantrums." Shaking his head in disbelief, "But I am a greater fool still, to allow you over my threshold at all!" The scandalised gasps of the ladies present only served to incense him further, and he pointed next at Anthony and Randolph, who were staring at him in astonishment. "And *you* two! Why can't you make yourselves useful? Find a profession, a wife, find *something*! Anthony, Mother still manages the estate at Huntingsend, because *you* have never exerted yourself to the task, and Randolph, you will run this family to ruin with your extravagance!"

"Giles, think of what you are saying," Clarissa began, rising from her chair with her embroidery still in her hands, but her brother shook his head.

"This is *my* house, Clarissa, and if you cannot understand that, perhaps you would be better off managing your own affairs in Camden Place instead of interfering in mine. I will not tolerate this foolishness any longer." With that, Sir Giles Kensington turned on his heel and marched out of the drawing room.

The house was utterly silent around him as he strode down the echoing corridor, hurried down the grand stairs and stomped into the hall. Footsteps sounded behind him as he reached the vestibule, and he looked around, expecting to see one of the servants, only for his gaze to land on Lady Annabella Harcourt instead.

"No scolding for me, Kensington?" she asked, eyebrows raised.

"Do not test me," he snapped. "And you have no right to address me in that impertinent way, after all the trouble you have caused me. At least the others are family, but *you*... I rue the day I promised my father I would look after you."

Lady Annabella did not so much as blink, calmly handing him his cloak and top hat. "But that's just it. Everyone upstairs in that room: they are your family, and it is your duty to tolerate them, no matter how trying they might be."

"Don't talk to me of duty." Sir Giles turned one hand on the door handle.

His ward's voice was so quiet that he almost did not hear it as he opened the front door to blinding sunlight. "They look to you, Kensington. We all do."

Sir Giles ignored her, seething, as he strode down the steps of No. 12 Cheltenham Place. An afternoon of peace and quiet, in one of his clubs: he had more than earned that, surely. The only question was whether he would be able to compose himself enough to enjoy his pipe and paper; he did not recall every feeling so angry in his life. He was so angry that he did not so much as tip his hat at the pale gentleman who came up to him on the pavement and asked if the house behind him was the residence of the earl of Langley.

"Yes, yes," he said crossly, "but he is not at home. Good day."

The sun sank over the rooftops of London. It had been a hot, heavy day, but under the growing dark, the streets cooled, and so did Sir Giles's temper. He had spent hours walking, and was just settling down to his dinner in one of the clubs when something struck him. In an instant he was up on his feet, the chair scraping back on the floor with an awful screech, and his eminent peers staring at him as he rushed out of the dining room.

A hansom cab brought him back to No. 12, and he overpaid the driver as he jumped out. It was now fully dark, and light gleamed in the upper windows of the townhouse, but no one came to greet him. There was only Tom Turner, sloping past with his head down, and Sir Giles grabbed hold of his shoulders, wild with worry.

"Tell me, Tom, has anything happened?"

"Oh, my lord," the stable boy stammered, his eyes wide. "There was a terrible scene!" Sir Giles's heart skipped a beat. "A man came into the house - he was looking for Lord Randolph, sir, and wouldn't take no for an answer. The maids were awful scared, and they went hiding with the ladies, watching from the landing above. Well, his Lordship came down to face him - "

"- Lord Randolph?" Sir Giles interrupted.

"- yes, Lord Randolph, sir, and he said he hadn't got the money, and then the gentleman wasn't very happy, and he said he was armed, and Lord Randolph said he was, too…"

"- with my pistol, no doubt," Sir Giles murmured to himself.

"And then Mr. Pearce sent me to get the watchman, so I didn't see what happened, but Adelaide called me back when I got a little ways down the street, and she tells me that Mr. Eaton has taken care of everything."

"Mr. *Eaton?*" Sir Giles was much impressed.

"Yes, sir." The boy looked relieved when he was let go, and ran off into the darkness. Walking slowly, the earl made his way back into his house.

He was assailed by his sister as soon as he stepped into the hallway. "Oh, Giles, I thought we would never see you again!" Alicia exclaimed as she planted a kiss on his cheek, her eyes shining. "It was simply horrible!" Turning to her husband, who stood apart, a little sheepish, "But Tobias saved us all, didn't you, my dear? He sent the scoundrel running."

Swallowing, Sir Giles turned to his brother-in-law and shook his hand. "Then I am in your debt."

"Well, now, I was only doing my duty," was Mr. Eaton's halting reply, and when Alicia had rushed upstairs to tell the others of their brother's return, he stepped towards Sir Giles, his eyes darting this way and that. "You may... er - tell your butler not to trouble himself about the carriage in the stables - and not to interfere if some men come to take it away."

"Ah, I see." Sir Giles's eyes lit with sudden comprehension. "A hundred guineas, did you say?"

"Yes, that fellow Tolbrook got quite a bargain." Mr. Eaton looked down, and coughed. "Well, since my Alicia has forsaken all earthly possessions, I thought it the best thing to do..."

"And is all forgiven?" But Sir Giles's question was answered as his sister poked her head over the staircase and trilled,

"Tobias! Come up to see Annabella, dear! She's simply *splendid*."

Her obedient husband trotted up to her, but Sir Giles Kensington remained where he was at the bottom of the stairs. Since leaving the dining club, he had experienced a sequence of powerful emotions, but one had prevailed over all the others. Now, though there was no longer any reason for it, the fear overwhelmed him, gripping every fiber of his being, until he glimpsed her at the top of the stairs, alive and well.

Then, as Lady Annabella Harcourt descended the stairs towards him, one gliding step at a time, his fear was replaced by something else entirely. Sir Giles Kensington gazed up at her, taking it all in: the white gloved hand that trailed along the banister, the red hair that had been swept up above her head so that only a few curls escaped, the gown whose substance more closely resembled that of a floating cloud than anything else. But what filled him with warmth was her smile when she reached him, the smile that faced all of his temper and forgave it.

Sir Giles was quiet as he took his ward's hand and escorted her out of Cheltenham Place. He was quiet for the whole evening that followed. The room at Almack's was perfectly appointed: there was an ideal number of couples, the musicians played well, and the supper that followed the dance in one of the adjoining rooms was satisfactory. Those were the only details that entered Sir Giles's consciousness, for to everyone else but Annabella he was utterly blind.

She was everywhere he looked: smiling and curtseying as she was presented to the finest families in London, dancing with a succession of gentlemen, none of whom seemed to be able to take their eyes off her. They were drawn to her like a moth to a candle flame, and Sir Giles felt that pull, too, as he never had before. It was for that reason that he kept himself apart as much as he could, and he could have cursed his sister Clarissa when she insisted, at the end of the night, that he escort Annabella home in his own carriage.

His ward was full of lively chatter, and Sir Giles let it wash over him as he peered out the window, lost in his own thoughts. He only allowed himself to look at her at last when she said, "I was sorry you did not dance." Leaning forward, she rested her elbows on her lap as she smiled mischievously at him. "I was saving the last one for you, you know."

"You had plenty of partners," he replied. "And my dancing days are over."

"But you dance so well! And thirty is not so very old, you know." Annabella laughed at his pained expression, and then, in a flash of white, jumped up from her seat and planted herself beside him instead. "I can help you find a nice young lady."

Momentarily overwhelmed by her closeness, Sir Giles turned back to look out at the lamplit streets.

"Don't ruin your gown," he said at last. "It cost me most of the Kensington family fortune."

"I thought Randolph cost you that," Annabella teased, and then, with another laugh, she put a hand on his arm. "Are you repenting your little tantrum yet?"

Sir Giles turned towards her, and had the satisfaction of seeing her eyes widen in surprise as he said quietly, "Yes." He hardly knew what he was thinking as he covered her hand with his. "I was worried, Annabella. Very worried."

There was a pause, and then their fingers twined together. She was very close now, and quiet, but her eyes held his, deep and inviting, and Sir Giles might very well have done something impetuous and impossible, had the coach's call not reminded him of where they were. He dropped Annabella's hand as the carriage came to a halt, and he looked away. Clearing his throat, "I'm glad you are safe."

"Well," she said, with a hard quality to her voice that had not been there before, "You will not have to worry about me for much longer. God willing, I shall be married before the end of the season."

"Annabella," Sir Giles said gently, but she ignored him, stepping out on her own.

9

ALL'S WELL THAT ENDS WELL

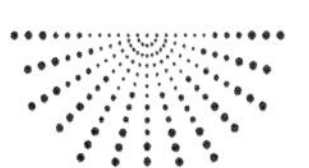

Lord Anthony Kensington was not an early riser by nature, but it was his belief that in the pursuit of true love, one could become a great many things. As such, the morning after Lady Annabella's debut, he rose by the clock, dressed and was out the door just as the servants were beginning to stir, and the rest of his family were still fast asleep in their beds. Up and down the lane outside Cheltenham Place he strolled, pen and paper in his hand and his brow furrowed deeply as he composed.

Back in the house, he waited at the bottom of the main staircase in the hall. The course of a week living close to his true love had taught him many things; he knew now that dear Adelaide was deeply shy and easily alarmed. That, of course, was why she avoided him at every turn in the house - although she had been bold enough when he had met her last night in the kitchen yard to ask him what his true intentions were. The sudden thought struck Anthony and gave him momentary puzzlement before he moved on, for coming down the stairs now was one of the housemaids. He promptly handed her the note, fixed her with an earnest look of entreaty which he was sure would not be ignored, and then went about his business.

Martha came into the servants' hall at a slow walk, her note folded behind her back. "Mrs. Deets," she said with careful consideration, watching the cook stoke the fire. "Why do you think the Adelaide girl's such a favourite with the folks upstairs?"

Mrs. Deets sighed and straightened, wiping her blackened hands on her apron. "I don't know, I'm sure. The master has some interest in her. But she ain't one of us, that much I can tell you. Not she, nor *that woman.*" With a darkly significant look, she flourished behind her with the poker. "An hour now since she went out to buy soap. Gossiping with Mrs. Hodges, more like. Always upon the gad, that one. One of us is packing our bags soon, Martha - oh, no, don't tell me 'tis her."

The two women turned towards the door at the sound of a brisk knocking. Mrs. Deets went to open it, and hastily put down the poker as she was handed an envelope by a messenger. With a look of surprise, she turned and held it out to Martha. "For you, dearie."

With greedy hands, Martha the housemaid seized the envelope, opened it, and turned so pale when she read the letter that Mrs. Deets had to fetch her a chair.

Upstairs in the breakfast room, an hour later, Lady Clarissa frowned over the rack of burnt toast, opened her mouth, and then closed it again.

"There has been a bit of an upheaval downstairs," Sir Giles explained. He, Clarissa and Anthony were the only ones at table. "One of the maids has received bad news. A great-aunt passed away, or so I understand."

"I'm sure I'm very sorry for her," his sister murmured. "However, in Camden Place, a neglect of duties… but I would not interfere for the world."

Sir Giles smiled as he recalled his words to Clarissa the day before. His smile slowly faded as he looked down the table. "Where are the others?"

It was Anthony who answered him. "Randolph and Annabella went out earlier, without taking breakfast."

"Out where?" Sir Giles demanded, and then, seeing the looks exchanged by brother and sister, cleared his throat. "I mean - that is, I'm sure they may do as they like…"

"Annabella was positively radiant last night," Clarissa remarked, after a short pause, and Sir Giles busied himself with cutting up his ham before replying.

"People appeared to be pleased with her."

"That should come as no surprise. Annabella has a great many fine qualities, and it is time you recognised them." As her brother lifted his head to glare at her, Clarissa continued, in gentler tones, "Did you two quarrel?"

"That is none of your…" Then, deflating somewhat, Sir Giles sighed, putting his knife down. "Annabella has a - a most aggravating habit of deliberately misunderstanding me."

"Then perhaps you had better set her right," his sister said carefully, but before he could answer her, Anthony interrupted.

"Dear brother, I may be younger than you in years, but in the realm of romance, I do count myself as an authority." Ignoring his brother's scoff, he set his chin on his hand as though deep in thought. "When you love a young lady, the only way to be sure that she may return your affections is to declare it as often as possible, and in as many ways as you can think of. You cannot expect her to reach the conclusion herself. She must be helped along... she must be encouraged, she must be... *Mother!*"

That last exclamation escaped him as, in the midst of his speech, the door of the breakfast room was thrown open and into their midst strode Lady Louisa Kensington. The gentlemen rose to their feet, and then Alfred tripped in after the new arrival, panting, "The - the Dowager Countess, my lords and ladies - "

"They know who I am," Lady Louisa snapped, shooing the footman out. As the door closed after him, she fixed her eldest son with a stare. "I would not wait for your servant. You know I detest town, but I came express from Langley, because I have something of great importance to tell you."

"Oh, Mother!" exclaimed Lord Anthony, as he rushed around the end of the table to come to her side. "You must forgive me for abandoning you without leaving a note, but I simply could not stay in Huntingsend after meeting Adelaide, knowing she was so far away…"

"Sit down, Anthony," the Dowager Countess said flatly. "This does not concern you." She looked back at Sir Giles. "But it does concern the girl, Adelaide, whom you wanted to present to me the day you visited Huntingsend."

"Mother," Sir Giles said quickly, though his heart was thumping in eagerness to hear her information, as he glanced at Clarissa and Anthony. "Had we not better retire to the library or…"

"I will tell you now," said Lady Louisa, "Or never." Her eyes fixed on her son, and he was shocked to see tears shining in their depths. "I did recognise that girl, Adelaide. I would have recognised her anywhere. She is the very picture of her mother. My sister."

There was a gasp among the three siblings. Ignoring their reactions, the Dowager Countess carried on as she began to stride up and down. "Twenty years ago, my sister Adela fell in love when she was at school, with the son of a clergyman who often visited there. He was poor, with no connections, and only a pleasing person to recommend him. My parents did not approve, but in time they might have allowed the match." With a significant look at Anthony, "However, Adela was of a romantic nature, and did not wait. She and this young man eloped, and were very happy for a short time, I believe, until he perished a few months into the marriage. He was consumptive."

"How dreadful," Lady Clarissa murmured again, and Sir Giles remained silent, unable to drag his eyes away from their mother.

"Adela was, by this time, in an interesting condition. She had no money, but she declared she would not return to Mamma and Papa, and so…" Lady Louisa sighed, and stopped short for a moment. "So I went to her, and nursed her until it was her time. She had a daughter, and fell ill. Towards the end of her sickness, she was in a high fever, and speaking a lot of nonsense - so I suppose I should not have promised her what I did. But with her last breath, Adela implored me not to bring her little girl back to our parents. I was reluctant to break my promise. Not only was my honour engaged, but my duty to my parents; I knew that the scandal following the news of the girl's birth might be too much for them. So I took the babe, named her Adelaide after her mother, and left her in a nearby tavern, with enough money to sustain her, and a necklace to tell her of her family, even if no one else could."

Tears were shining in Lady Clarissa's eyes when her mother finished her account; Sir Giles felt similarly overcome, but it was their brother Anthony whose reaction was the most violent of all. He had gone white, and with a cry of agony, he ran out of the room.

"Oh, well," the Dowager Countess said, some of her old dryness returning, "I suppose that little romance is over."

"Adelaide is upstairs, attending Alicia," Lady Clarissa said quietly as she rose to her feet. "I will go fetch her."

"I'll come with you," said her mother unexpectedly. "Well, I can't be seen to ignore any of my children, can I? Alicia might feel slighted."

When they had left, Sir Giles sank down into his chair and slowly dropped his head into his hands. With the mystery of Adelaide's person solved, he ought to have felt that a great burden had lifted from his shoulders, but something remained: a question which had been plaguing his mind for some time now.

He was still in that attitude when the door of the breakfast room opened once more. The light, graceful step of Lady Annabella required no confirming glance, but all the same, Sir Giles could not resist. He raised his head and saw her standing opposite the table. She was wearing one of her day gowns, the green one which made her look like a woodland sprite. The strings of her bonnet still hung about her neck, and she began to untie them as she addressed her guardian. "Kensington, whatever's the matter?"

"Nothing; nothing," Sir Giles said as he got to his feet.

"Good, because I have a favour to ask you." She paused as though uncertain - though with Annabella, that could not be possible - and then began, "Randolph and I have just been to see the Longstone regiment marching out. It was his idea, but as we were standing there on Bond Street, *I* had a thought. What if you were to purchase a military commission for Randolph?"

Sir Giles frowned, slowly rising from his seat. "So you are suggesting that I spend even more money..."

"Money will be spent in any case, if you allow Randolph to return to Oxford again," Annabella said calmly, turning to follow him as he walked around the breakfast table. "You *know* he cannot resist a good game. But soldiering would suit him, and he has an interest in it. It might turn out to give him the discipline he needs."

With his back to her now, Sir Giles shook his head. "I know Randolph better than you, Annabella, and there is no way that he could bear the life of a soldier."

"I think you underestimate his fortitude."

"And I think *you* overestimate my generosity." Sir Giles turned again, and Annabella took a step towards him, her hands folded before her breast in a gesture of supplication. The thought of what might have effected this sudden show of humility made something ache within him. "My brother is lucky indeed to have such a friend as you."

Annabella flinched at the jibe, but carried on nonetheless, "So you will do it? You will give him a commission?"

"How can I refuse you anything?" Sir Giles spread his hands, summoning as much venom into his voice as possible. "It is done. And if you have any other favour to ask of me…"

"What else could there be? I do this to help *you*." At her guardian's disbelieving laugh, Annabella moved even closer to him, a coldness entering her tone. "But I see that is not your view. Tell me, Kensington, what other motive can I have in helping your brother?"

In growing confusion, Sir Giles cleared his throat. "Well, it is clear to me…"

"Yes?" Lady Annabella Harcourt's green eyes did not leave his. She was almost upon him now. Sir Giles coughed again, and then, as the door opened behind him, he turned to greet the new arrival with some relief.

"Mrs. Deets. What can I do for you?"

"My lord, if I may ask you a favour…"

"A favour?" Sir Giles raised his eyebrows at Annabella, who had come level with him. "Indeed." His ward glowered. Uncertain, the cook glanced between them, before resuming,

"I have heard the good news about Lady Adelaide, my lord, and we are all very happy downstairs. And since all"s prepared for her departure with the Dowager Countess to Huntingsend, along with Mrs. Higgenbotham…"

"Is it?" Sir Giles folded his arms, the picture of ease. "Well, my mother is full of surprises."

"... it means we'll be short a few hands downstairs."

"Of course," Annabella said, so quietly that Sir Giles did not hear her - but Mrs. Deets did, and for the first time she smiled, her round face transforming in the action.

"And as we cannot always rely on Lady Annabella to help..."

Confused, Sir Giles frowned, opened his mouth, and then closed it again.

"... it's my humble request that Mrs. Higgenbotham be allowed to remain here with us."

Amazed, the seventh earl of Langley did nothing but stare at his cook for a moment. "But... but you and she..."

"We may not always see eye to eye," said Mrs. Deets firmly, "But she is a good cook, too, and, I believe, will help me to better myself."

Much struck, Sir Giles was silent for a moment. At last, he ventured, "That's very... er... noble of you, Mrs. Deets, but are you quite sure..."

"Of course she must stay," Annabella interrupted him. "I will go downstairs with you now, Mrs. Deets, and tell her myself."

"My lady, you're very kind but you needn't - "

"Annabella!" Incensed, Sir Giles followed at a quick stride after his ward as she began to lead their cook out of the breakfast room. "I believe *I* shall decide whether Mrs. Higgenbotham stays or goes."

Annabella ignored him as they crossed the foyer. "My lady." Mrs. Deets protested. "I'm sure I can pass on the message to Mrs. Higgenbotham: I wouldn't want to put you out of your way - "

"Nonsense! Come along, Kensington." This last command Lady Annabella Harcourt threw over her shoulder before following Mrs. Deets downstairs.

A shouting reached their ears as they entered the servants' hall, and they were greeted with a surprising scene: the ever-composed Mr. Pearce was red in the face as he paced up and down by the dining table, his hands folded behind his back, Sal Higgenbotham was sitting at the head, an expression of delight on her face, while Alfred and Tom Turner peered over her shoulder at the note in her hand.

"She is but a servant! She has no fortune, no breeding, and clearly no sense! It is a connection that will only bring disgrace and infamy to the Kensingtons. It is an outrage!"

"I said it, Mr. Pearce," said Sal Higgenbotham placidly. "I always said she was a deep one, that girl."

"You never said nothing of the sort, Sal," Mrs. Deets burst out, and then reddened. Her fellow servants, by contrast, went pale as they saw who had just entered.

"What," said Sir Giles Kensington in a slow, dangerous voice, "is the meaning of this, Mr. Pearce? Am I to understand that you look upon the addition of Adelaide Coventry to our family as an outrage?"

The butler blinked at him in uncomprehension. "Miss Adelaide… my lord, I don't understand."

"It's Martha we were speaking of, not Adelaide, my lord," Sal Higgenbotham said helpfully, before Sir Giles could open his mouth again. She indicated the note in her hand. "She's only gone and eloped."

"Eloped?" Sir Giles repeated. He glanced at Lady Annabella, whose expression was unreadable. "With whom?"

The combined antics of Alicia, Randolph and Annabella had never produced such a shock as the residents of No. 12 Cheltenham Place experienced that day. Sir Giles fared somewhat better than his mother, who fainted dead away when the note was recovered in Lord Anthony's room. She was revived by smelling salts and the attentions of her pug, but it was some hours before she could speak. The ladies of the household stayed with her, and occasional reports on her progress were brought to Sir Giles as he sat at his writing desk in the library.

A clear picture of what had happened began to emerge, following interviews of varying usefulness with Mr. Pearce, Mrs. Deets and Mrs. Higgenbotham. Sir Giles at last gathered that on hearing of Adelaide's true origins, his brother Anthony had found himself compelled to transfer his affections to another young woman of a similar type. In one respect, however, Martha was different from Anthony's past loves, as it was now discovered that the venerable relation whose passing had disrupted their breakfast, had also left to her great-niece the considerable fortune of ten thousand pounds.

"There is some comfort in that," said Lady Clarissa, when she came down to the library to speak with her brother. It was dark now, and the lamps had been lit. "At least Anthony will have something: for Mother says the estate must be left in your hands, now, Giles."

"It was always to be my lot," Sir Giles said wearily. He placed one hand on his temple and rubbed it, taking a break for a moment from the letter he was writing. "Though I had hoped Anthony would settle there, it is impossible now."

"But Huntingsend is no bachelor's residence," Lady Clarissa said, with a significant look. "You will need a mistress."

"There is a mistress."

"Mother doesn't count." They both turned as the door opened, and in strode Lady Annabella Harcourt. Sir Giles put down his pen and raised his eyebrows, while Clarissa murmured an excuse and tiptoed out of the room.

"Well? Where have you been through all this chaos?"

"Helping Randolph to pack his things," Annabella said cheerfully, coming to sit in the spot Clarissa had just vacated opposite his desk. "You will be glad to hear that I have forgiven you."

"Forgiven - what -? " Sir Giles spluttered.

"And I have some very good suggestions as to how to manage this new situation."

"Well, by all means." Sir Giles leaned his chin on his hand and gestured for her to continue.

"Give Lady Louisa a little time, and then allow Anthony back into the fold. He may take over Huntingsend with Martha by his side, and you needn't budge from Cheltenham Place."

"Impossible," he said at once.

"Do you doubt that your mother will forgive Anthony? He is her favourite, isn't he?"

"Yes, but…"

"Kensington." Lady Annabella Harcourt leaned forward over the desk, her green eyes intent on his. "There have been far more disparate matches, and the world is changing. Martha is no longer a servant, she is an heiress." At his silence, she leaned back in her chair, with a satisfied expression.

Sir Giles did not reply for a moment. She watched him, and for a long moment they sat opposite one another without speaking. At last, very quietly, "Far more disparate matches, you say."

"Yes, and you know it to be true, Kensington - "

"What if a guardian were to fall in love with his ward? What would you say to that?"

Annabella had gone very still. Sir Giles's eyes found her face, but she looked down at her lap, her eyelashes dark on her cheeks. "What would you say," he went on softly, "if he told you that he did not intend for it to happen? That he did not realise the danger he was in until it was too late? That he found himself jealous of his brother, jealous of every man who looked at her at Almack's?"

She did not speak, or look at him. His voice dropped to a whisper. "Annabella! If you do not wish me to go on, you must tell me now. Otherwise…"

Annabella finally raised her eyes to his. Her lips barely parted as she said, "Otherwise?"

Sir Giles's heart was thumping as he stood from his desk and moved to her side, as he knelt and gently took her trembling hand, pressed it to his lips.

"Yes." It was barely more than a breath in his ear; he thought he must have imagined it until Annabella's arms went around his neck, and then he had her in a close embrace, his cheek pressed to hers, and a wild delight was thrilling through him. "My answer is yes."

"I didn't ask you anything yet," Sir Giles felt compelled to point out after a minute or two spent in this pleasant fashion, and instantly regretted his words as Annabella detached herself from him.

"Quite right." With a rustling of skirts, she stood, and Sir Giles, still kneeling, gazed up at her. "So I will save you the trouble. Yes, Kensington, I will marry you."

Laughing, the seventh earl of Langley stood and took his lady in his arms again. She turned her face up to his obligingly, and he had just pressed a kiss on her lips when they heard a knock on the library door, and through the wood the sound of Lord Randolph's impatient voice. "Can we come in yet?"

"Yes," Sir Giles called reluctantly after a moment, and then stared to see his entire family piling in through the door: Randolph was followed by Alicia, Tobias and Clarissa, and last of all was the Dowager Countess, arm in arm with Adelaide. The chatter and laughter soon filled the air, and Sir Giles and Annabella had their hands clasped in turn by each of their family.

Only Lady Louisa seemed incapable of smiling, her swollen eyes and trembling arms bespeaking the shock she had recently received. She did not speak again until they were all seated at dinner, when the time came to raise a toast.

"This has been a day of joy and sadness," she said gravely. "I have lost a son - pug, *behave* - but I have also found a daughter." She turned to Adelaide, whose eyes shone at her great-aunt.

"*Two* daughters," Lady Annabella Harcourt corrected.

The Dowager Countess gave a reluctant smile. "Quite right, Annabella. And to think, it all came from your running off to Gretna Green."

THANK YOU FOR CHOOSING A PUREREAD BOOK!

We hope you enjoyed the story, and as a way to thank you for choosing PureRead we'd like to send you this free book, and other fun reader rewards…

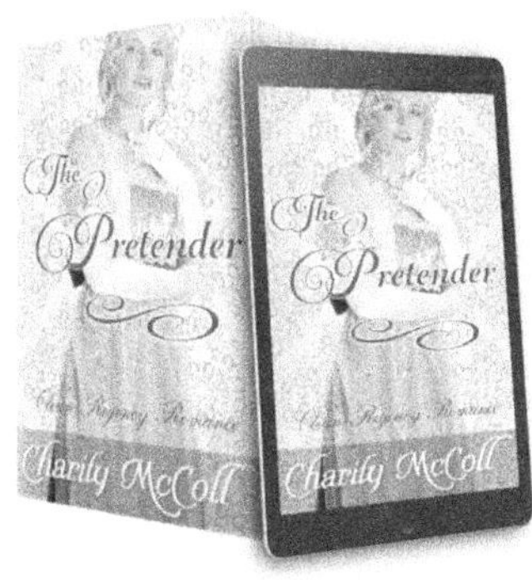

An undercover plan designed to win a young nobleman's heart is threatened when the lovely Gabrielle Belgrade's soft conscience and honesty threatens to undo the matchmaking shenanigans of Lord Grant's well intentioned godmother.

Click here for your free copy of The Pretender
PureRead.com/regency

Thanks again for reading.
See you soon!

Be the first to know when we release new books, take part in our fun competitions, and get surprise free books in your inbox by signing up to our free VIP Reader list.

As a thank you you'll receive a copy of *The Pretender* straight away in you inbox.

Click here for your free copy of The Pretender

PureRead.com/regency